D1191852

Looking at Mesopotamian Myths and Legends

THE HERO KING
GILGAMESH

Irving Finkel

 **NTC** *NTC Publishing Group*
Lincolnwood, Illinois USA

Irving Finkel is a curator in the Department of Western Asiatic Antiquities, British Museum. He is the author of several books for children including *The Lewis Chessmen and What Happened to Them*. He has written all the cuneiform signs used in this book.

The photomicrographs on the front cover and on pages 1, 6, 23 and 29 were produced by Margaret Sax and Nigel Meeks in the Department of Scientific Research and the images processed by Tony Milton, Photographic Services, in the British Museum. This is the first time that these photomicrographs have been published.

Published by NTC Publishing Group
4255 West Touhy Avenue
Lincolnwood (Chicago)
Illinois 60646-1975
USA

First published in the United Kingdom in 1998 by
British Museum Press

Irving Finkel has asserted his right to be identified as the Author of this work

**Library of Congress Cataloguing in Publication Data
is available from the Library of Congress**

ISBN 0-8442-4701-4

Designed by Carla Turchini
Printed in Hong Kong

Front cover: Photomicrograph of a hero figure from a bloodstone cylinder seal.
Title page: Photomicrograph of the head of a lion carved on a cylinder seal. This area of the carving is less than half an inch square.

CONTENTS

ABOUT GILGAMESH

Gilgamesh, the hero of this story, was once a real king in the land of ancient Mesopotamia (now modern Iraq). He ruled in the great city of Uruk, and must have lived in about 2700 BC. So much happened to him during his life that afterwards many stories and myths were composed about him by court poets and singers.

Originally these stories circulated by word of mouth. They were recited round the fire, deep into the night, but for hundreds of years they were never written down. Some storytellers told them in the ancient Sumerian language, some in ancient Babylonian. It is easy to imagine children in those days, wide-eyed as they listened to the dramatic events concerning gods and heroes that had been handed down from such remote times.

The story in this book is the version of Gilgamesh's adventures that was discovered in the 19th century in the library of Assurbanipal, King of Assyria. This was a library not of books, but of clay tablets, impressed with an ancient form of writing called cuneiform. These clay tablets were written in the seventh century BC, over two and a half thousand years ago. The story tells of one of the great friendships of all time, and how Gilgamesh came to seek the elusive secret of eternal life.

The great Assyrian king Assurbanipal. This scene of the king at a lion hunt is carved on a stone relief that decorated his royal palace. Assurbanipal lived in the seventh century BC, some 2,000 years later than Gilgamesh himself, but tablets with this heroic story were prized by the king.

One of King Assurbanipal's clay tablets. It contains part of the Gilgamesh story, written in cuneiform script. This tablet was broken in ancient times – scholars still hope to find the missing parts.

Cuneiform is the oldest writing known. It was developed in Mesopotamia long before Gilgamesh was born, probably about 3200 BC. The cuneiform signs were impressed into clay tablets with a special tool. The signs were not letters, like our alphabet, but stood for syllables, such as En-ki-du, Hum-ba-ba and Ish-tar.

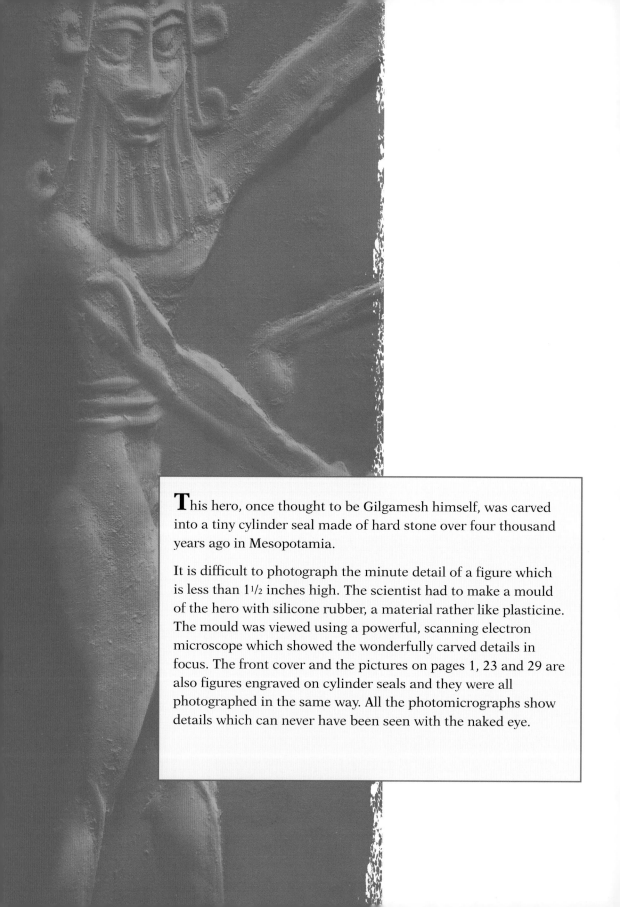

This hero, once thought to be Gilgamesh himself, was carved into a tiny cylinder seal made of hard stone over four thousand years ago in Mesopotamia.

It is difficult to photograph the minute detail of a figure which is less than 1½ inches high. The scientist had to make a mould of the hero with silicone rubber, a material rather like plasticine. The mould was viewed using a powerful, scanning electron microscope which showed the wonderfully carved details in focus. The front cover and the pictures on pages 1, 23 and 29 are also figures engraved on cylinder seals and they were all photographed in the same way. All the photomicrographs show details which can never have been seen with the naked eye.

GILGAMESH MEETS ENKIDU

Long ago, in the far-distant world of ancient Mesopotamia, there once lived (as we can read to this day) a quite remarkable king. Gilgamesh was his name, and he was king in the city of Uruk. Like all famous kings he was, of course, tall and strong and wise and handsome. His poets described him as a hero, and a goring wild bull, and asked of themselves "who can compare with him in kingliness?" This was really an unanswerable question because, unlike most kings of whom stories are told, Gilgamesh was two-thirds god and one-third man. His mother was the goddess Ninsun, sometimes called Rimat-Ninsun. His father, on the other hand, was human.

Gilgamesh underwent great and famous adventures. He traveled fearlessly through great perils and battled tirelessly against what seemed hopeless odds. His proud scribes who lived in Uruk squatted on their haunches and wrote down the story on tablets of clay, and sometimes, with an eye to the future, on rare tablets of beautiful lapis lazuli, brought from afar. "Open the box," they say, "undo the fastening of its secret opening, and read for yourself how Gilgamesh endured every hardship in triumph."

Uruk was a remarkable city, spacious and massive in its architecture, with towering walls of brick that could be seen by a traveler from far off through the haze. The inhabitants were proud of their walls, which they thought the ancient Seven Sages had designed. They were proud, too, of the temples, especially the holy Eanna, where the famous goddess Ishtar lived. Ishtar was a complex and unpredictable character. She was in charge of love and war at the same time, and has a lot to do with this story.

At the beginning of this story King Gilgamesh was restless and bored. He wandered around Uruk, disturbing people, interrupting them about their business and even interfering with marriage ceremonies and other celebrations. The people became distressed, because although they were ready to do anything for Gilgamesh, and were as loyal as they could be, he was, to tell the truth, getting to be a bit of a nuisance.

Some citizens in particular, sorely provoked by the king's behavior, were moved to make a serious complaint to the gods in heaven about him. Their message reached Anu, who was king of the gods, and also, by the way, Ishtar's father. Anu felt that their point was reasonable, and had a word with Aruru, the plump mother-goddess who had helped make Gilgamesh so handsome and talented and strong. Anu suggested that she produce a rival to Gilgamesh, a strong and pugnacious character who would prove to be a distraction and a challenge, so that Gilgamesh would leave everyone else in peace.

Aruru responded without hesitation. First (you will be pleased to hear), as befits a creator-goddess, she washed her hands. Then she pinched off some clay, the material which the Mesopotamians always put to such good use, and tossed it down into the wild country near Uruk, this time using it to manufacture a decidedly remarkable being.

His name was Enkidu. He was tall and strong, but most noticeably he was very hairy, with long flowing locks about his head, and hair all over his body too. Although he looked like a man, albeit a wild and naked one, he lived like an animal. He ran fleetly and lived off grass with the gazelles. When he was thirsty he competed for a place at the water hole with all the other animals, who considered him (if they stopped to think about it) one of themselves. Enkidu roamed around energetically, enjoying life in an unthinking kind of way.

One day a professional animal trapper who lived near Uruk went on a hunting trip in the countryside. All of a sudden he came face to face with Enkidu at the water hole. The sight gave him a tremendous shock, and he could hardly move for sheer terror. Once he regained control of his legs he rushed straight home. His father could tell at once from his son's face that

NATURAL
MAN

something terrible had happened. The trapper did his best to describe the awful vision, complaining how Enkidu filled in the pits that he had dug, and rescued animals from his traps, ruining his business. His father was a practical man, and he came up with a practical suggestion. He recommended putting the problem to king Gilgamesh.

Off went the trapper to Uruk. He explained the whole thing all over again to Gilgamesh, who knew exactly what to do. He told the trapper to find a certain young woman, famed for her attractiveness, who would make Enkidu fall in love with her, and so change him into a man like other men. This, Gilgamesh predicted, would have the effect of alienating all the animals from him. The name of this young woman was Shamhat.

The trapper found Shamhat, and they went off together on the trip, which took three days. They found the waterhole, and waited for Enkidu, which took another three days. Animals of all types arrived to drink, but in the end Enkidu turned up himself. Shamhat was taken aback at her first glimpse of him, so wild in appearance, and crouching to drink like a savage, but she acted upon her instructions. She drew the mesmerized Enkidu to her and kissed him.

Enkidu was transformed by her beauty and passion. As Gilgamesh had foreseen, the animals fled before him. His natural familiarity with them had vanished, and to all the wild species he was no longer one of them at all. Enkidu found that he could not run as fast as before, but on the other hand something else had changed. His mind had broadened, and his humanity had developed, and he listened carefully to what Shamhat had to say.

Shamhat told him that he had now become beautiful, that he was even like a god. His days of living with wild beasts, she said, were over. On the contrary, it was now time for him to leave the countryside for good and return with her to Uruk. She described to him the wonderful temples in the city, and the powerful gods who lived there. Rather cleverly she also talked about Gilgamesh, blessed by the gods. She mentioned how he thought himself the strongest man in the world, and how he strode about the city, filled with restless energy, with no one to challenge him. The message was not lost on Enkidu. His immediate decision was to take on Gilgamesh in a one-to-one

ENKIDU

contest. Shamhat tried to talk him out of it. She told Enkidu how the greatest gods in heaven themselves were interested in Gilgamesh, and always looked out for him. She told him that Gilgamesh even knew in advance that Enkidu was on his way. The king had already had special dreams about it, she told Enkidu.

In the first dream, Gilgamesh had seen a meteorite fall from heaven. It was indescribably heavy, and he had struggled to pick it up in front of all the people, but he was unable to move it at all. All the people were very impressed by the fact, and many kissed the great stone, and Gilgamesh too found himself embracing it. On waking he had been rather puzzled, but his wise mother Rimat-Ninsun knew the significance of the dream. It was a good dream, she said. The stone was a mighty man and fighter, and a comrade who would come to save Gilgamesh.

A similar dream soon followed, in which an axe appeared at the door, which Gilgamesh again found himself embracing. Rimat-Ninsun's explanation was the same. It was this mighty man, she said, the strongest in the land, who would come to save Gilgamesh.

As Shamhat must have expected, knowing about these dreams was the final straw. Enkidu was determined to meet this over-confident Gilgamesh for himself.

ENKIDU BECOMES HUMAN

Continues to Become Civilized

Once this was decided, things moved quickly. Shamhat realized that Enkidu could no longer go around naked, so she made a garment for him out of her own clothing. Under her influence Enkidu learned about proper food and drink. He was finding it much easier to get along with people. The shepherds saw that he must be the hero referred to in Gilgamesh's dream, and treated him with respect. In return Enkidu obligingly chased off wolves and lions so that the shepherds and their flocks could sleep at night.

Soon afterwards, while Emkidu and Shamhat were still lingering outside the city, a man appeared who was obviously in a great hurry. When they questioned him, he told them that he was going to a wedding. Gilgamesh was also going to be there, and he was boasting that he would carry the bride off for himself. The minute he heard this piece of outrageous news Enkidu became red with anger. He decided then and there to go to Uruk to deal with Gilgamesh, and off he strode, closely followed by Shamhat.

To great acclaim Enkidu marched down the street in Uruk. The people crowded around him, wanting to kiss his feet as in Gilgamesh's dream.

Enkidu stood solidly at the door to the marriage chamber, to prevent Gilgamesh from entering. As you can imagine, when Gilgamesh arrived a fight broke out between them, right then and there in the street. Onlookers described how the doorposts trembled and the walls shook, but in the middle of a wrestler's throw Gilgamesh suddenly felt his anger leave him, and he turned away. At that point Enkidu understood that the god Enlil had truly destined Gilgamesh for great kingship. He acknowledged Gilgamesh as his superior, and from that moment the two heroes were friends, destined to face the future as the closest of partners. Sharing such deep friendship was something new and wonderful for both. The city of Uruk was at their feet and they spent their days in great companionship and luxury.

After some time, however, Gilgamesh felt that they might both be getting a little weak. Life was too easy, and both needed a new challenge to invigorate them and test their powers to the full. It was under these circumstances that Gilgamesh came up with the idea of the Cedar Forest adventure.

It would be a hazardous journey to the Cedar Forest of Lebanon, but the real dangers would begin when they reached the Forest itself. The reason for this was the dreadful monster, Humbaba. His very roar was like a flood, his mouth like fire, his breath like death. The god Enlil had created him specially to be guardian of the Forest. As a result, Humbaba had unusually fine hearing which allowed him to hear rustling caused by intruders from even 100 leagues away. The minute he heard such a sound he would be there, and any mere human would be paralyzed with terror.

Like Gilgamesh, Enkidu had been grumbling that his arms were growing weak, and his strength slack, but he changed his tune when Gilgamesh started talking about this plan. Enkidu declared that it would be foolish to go anywhere near the Forest. Seeing this, Gilgamesh remarked sympathetically, "As for human beings, their days are numbered, and whatever they try to do is but wind," and proposed that he should go in front, so that Enkidu could stand safely behind, and yell out to him words of encouragement. "Should I fall," mused Gilgamesh out loud, "they will say it was Gilgamesh who took on the monster Humbaba in battle."

Enkidu rapidly put a stop to that kind of talk, and the two heroes resolved that they would face Humbaba together.

The first thing was to arm themselves with the best-quality and most reliable weapons suitable for heroes. They decided that they would each need an axe, a hatchet, a sword, and body armor. They explained their requirements to the city craftsmen, who discussed how they could manufacture what was needed.

The terrible face of Humbaba. This likeness of the monster was probably made in about 1700 BC.

Ancient Mesopotamians believed that experts could tell the future by examining the internal organs of a sacrificed sheep. This clay model shows a particular pattern that might turn up in a sheep's intestines, looking exactly like the face of Humbaba. We know that because it is written on the back in cuneiform. This model was made for teaching young apprentices.

Gilgamesh and Enkidu held a meeting to announce to the men of Uruk what they were intending to do, and why they were doing it, and ask them for their blessing. Gilgamesh declared that he would play his usual role in the New Year Festival before setting out on the journey.

Enkidu, however, was still plagued by doubts and fears, and he took the opportunity to speak to the assembled men of Uruk in the hope that they could dissuade Gilgamesh from this suicidal plan. His hopes rose when the city elders stood up to give Gilgamesh their opinion.

"You are young, Gilgamesh," they said, "you are impulsive. You do not know what you are talking about." In an attempt to frighten their king from his purpose, they proceeded to describe the awful Humbaba in the traditional way, emphasizing his famous roar, his awful mouth and his terrible breath, and what inevitably happened to human beings who confronted him.

Gilgamesh listened politely, but their words had no effect. He was determined to win eternal fame and honor in battle with Humbaba, or die in the attempt, and no one was going to stop him!

THEY PREPARE FOR THE CEDAR FOREST ADVENTURE

In the face of their king's determination there was little that the city elders could do. The best they managed was to insist that Enkidu should go in front while they were on the journey, since he knew the route. In fact they made poor Enkidu responsible for Gilgamesh, telling him that they expected him to bring Gilgamesh back safe and sound.

Despite his outward bravery, Gilgamesh himself was by no means free of apprehension and nervousness. He suggested to Enkidu that they go and see his mother, the goddess Ninsun, and ask her to intercede on their behalf with Shamash the Sun God. This would be a sensible plan, because Shamash was always concerned with justice and fair play, and they knew that he considered Humbaba an evil force in the world. Gilgamesh suggested that Ninsun might mention to Shamash that if they came back safely from their journey he and Enkidu would see to it that a special Shamash monument was put up in celebration.

Ninsun took this suggestion rather seriously, since she was worried about the outcome of her son's great adventure herself. She went to her quarters, and, taking a special plant that was famous for its magical powers, she washed herself, and dressed in a beautiful robe, with a sash, her jewels, and her divine crown on her head.

Ninsun, being a goddess, knew how to undertake this sort of negotiation properly. After offering a little water from a bowl, she went up onto the roof, and burned some incense to attract Shamash's attention. Raising her arms she pleaded with him eloquently. She asked why he had imposed such a restless heart on her son, making him determined to take such a dangerous path. She reminded Shamash that he himself loathed Humbaba, and wanted him destroyed. Ninsun also called on Aya, Shamash's own wife, to mention now and again to her husband that he might keep an eye on Gilgamesh and help him to return safely.

After this she turned to Enkidu, and welcomed him as if he were her own child. She gave him a special amulet, and declared to her priestesses and the women who surrounded her that she had taken Enkidu into her heart.

Many secret rites and magical precautions were then taken in the temples of Uruk to safeguard the adventurers in their hour of danger. After all the preparations had been completed the city elders reluctantly met once more to address the heroes. Some of them still had hopes of calling the whole thing off. Their final word was to Enkidu again, making him responsible for bringing back their king. Enkidu resolved to do his best, and the elders joined in wishing the heroes every success.

The god Shamash (in the center) emerges from the underworld, watched by other gods and goddesses.

This is a modern impression from an ancient seal. Seals were rolled over the surface of a clay tablet.

THEY JOURNEY TO THE CEDAR FOREST

So, at last, they were off. Feeling a sense of relief to be away from the endless discussions and elaborate preparations, Gilgamesh and Enkidu set out on the fateful road to the dreaded Cedar Forest. They were determined to cover the ground at breakneck speed, so it was a good twenty leagues before they even stopped for food, and another thirty before they stopped for the night. They kept up this rate of fifty leagues a day for three days, covering in that period a distance that would probably have taken a normal man a good month and a half.

On the third day they saw the Cedar Forest in the far distance. That night they worked together and dug a well pointing in the direction of the Sun God Shamash, as he was setting for the night. Gilgamesh climbed a nearby mountain, and offering some special flour as a symbolic gift, he appealed to the mountain to bring him a message from Shamash in a dream.

The two heroes then camped for the night. As Gilgamesh squatted down with his chin on his knees he fell into a deep sleep. In the morning he awoke in a strange state, trembling and deeply affected, and he scolded Enkidu for not waking him during the night. He confided the details of the dream he had just experienced to Enkidu, telling him of a mountain he had seen. Enkidu interpreted the dream for Gilgamesh, reassuring him that the mountain in the dream represented Humbaba, and that the remainder of the dream foretold their victory in the coming struggle.

This pattern was repeated exactly on the next day, with Gilgamesh and Enkidu pausing once for food but hardly pausing for breath as they covered fifty more leagues. Again that night Gilgamesh fell into a deep sleep, and experienced a second significant dream. In the morning he described to Enkidu how he had found himself grappling with a wild bull in the wilderness, a creature so fearsome that his very bellow could split the ground. Someone else in the dream had given Gilgamesh water to drink when he really needed it out of his own waterskin. Gilgamesh was inclined to think that this bull must be the foe that awaited them in the forest, but Enkidu realized that, on the contrary, it represented Shamash, while the god who had given him water was Lugalbanda, his own father.

This pattern was repeated for a third, a fourth, and a fifth time, and each night Gilgamesh experienced a prophetic dream. Each morning Enkidu, his friend and companion, explained the meaning of the dream. The third dream involved an earthquake and bolts of lightning, when death rained down and all was turned to ash. The fourth dream, in Enkidu's eyes, was clear message that they would defeat Humbaba, and the fifth dream was the same.

By this time the heroes were not far from the outskirts of the Cedar Forest. At one point Enkidu seemed to be on the point of losing his nerve. Gilgamesh recalled their agreement in Uruk, and tried to rally his flagging courage by quoting proverbs, remarking that "a slippery path is not feared by two who help each other," or "even a mighty lion can be rolled over by a pair of cubs." Gilgamesh reminded him of the great journey they had shared together, and of Enkidu's great valor in times of conflict. "Take my hand, my friend," he cried, "we will go on together. Your heart should burn to do battle ..."

Talking in this fashion, and moving onward, resolute in their friendship and loyalty, they realized suddenly that they had reached the edge of the dreaded forest. Falling silent they stood together, and gazed ahead.

THEY BATTLE WITH HUMBABA

Their first sight of the forest proved unexpected. It was, for one thing, truly beautiful, and beckoned to Gilgamesh and Enkidu with its luxurious greenery and well-shaded path after the rigors of the journey. The path led straight into the heart of the forest, and they strode along it together. On each side the vegetation seemed like dense matting. Before long they passed Cedar Mountain, which they knew to be a holy dwelling where a powerful goddess lived.

However, Humbaba knew of their arrival. Whether he would have sensed their presence merely from their footfalls on the forest floor cannot be known, but the heroes, prompted by a giddy sense of bravado, unsheathed their weapons and started cutting at the trees.

Up came Humbaba. At first, Humbaba tried to warn Gilgamesh and Enkidu off rather than fight. Perhaps the monster sensed that on this occasion his own terrible powers might not be sufficient, and that he might even be defeated. So Humbaba, terrible and fearsome to all who beheld him, tried to use words as his weapons.

First, he sneered at Gilgamesh for taking advice from such a character as Enkidu. How could Gilgamesh be led by such an idiot? Then he jeered at Enkidu. Humbaba knew all about Enkidu's humble origins among the animals and, quoting proverbs of his own, he recommended that Enkidu should save his advice for his friends the dumb animals, and cease to lead Gilgamesh astray. His anger rising, Humbaba threatened to feed Gilgamesh's flesh to the screeching vulture and the eagle.

The monster's next weapon was his own face. He began to make the most ferocious and distorted expressions. Gilgamesh

HUMBABA

was terrified, fearing that he would be bewitched, so he ran and hid. Enkidu rallied his friend by reminding him of their own great weapons, the best that could be procured from the craftsmen in Uruk, and the two heroes turned together to face Humbaba, once and for all.

The battle that followed can hardly be described. The ground itself split open as they stamped their feet, and the sky grew dark, so that the heroes found themselves enveloped in a deathly fog. Things looked terrifyingly dark and dangerous. It was at this point that Shamash, the Sun God, came to their aid. That well-timed appeal by Gilgamesh's mother Ninsun had not been in vain. Shamash immediately dispatched thirteen winds to fight at their side.

(Perhaps you didn't know that there could be as many as thirteen separate winds? Well, first of course there are the South, North, East and West Winds, but in an emergency a worried Sun God in ancient Mesopotamia could also call on

Gilgamesh and Enkidu's battle with Humbaba, carved on a seal. The carver has shown the giant Humbaba kneeling down, so that he can fit into the small space. You can see how Humbaba appears back to front on the seal and the right way around on the seal impression.

This part of the Gilgamesh story must have been well-known and popular in ancient Mesopotamia because versions of the scene are carved on many ancient seals.

the Whistling Wind, the Biting Wind, the Blizzard, the Evil Wind, the Simurru Wind, the Demon Wind, the Ice Wind, not to mention the Storm and the Sandstorm, to help him out.)

These magnificent winds swirled violently about Humbaba, buffetting him this way and that so that he could hardly move, let alone escape. This meant that Gilgamesh could get close enough to him to use his weapons. He raised his arm high to sweep off the monster's head when Humbaba spoke out, begging for mercy. Flattering the youthful Gilgamesh, and blaming the whole affair on the troublemaker Shamash, Humbaba offered to serve him well, putting the resources of his forest at Gilgamesh's disposal. In alarm, Enkidu shouted at Gilgamesh not to listen to Humbaba, but to kill him quickly.

Again Humbaba spoke up, asking for mercy, this time addressing himself to Enkidu. Defending the forest was his job, he argued, as decreed by the gods, so he was really only doing his duty, and while he could have killed them both at once, he had tried to persuade them to leave quietly. In view of this, he said, his own life should now be spared. Enkidu was unmoved by such arguments, and again cried to Gilgamesh to finish the job, to smash Humbaba and pulverize him into little bits. This frantic dispute continued for some time, with the formidable guardian thinking up different arguments, and Enkidu overriding him, until Humbaba uttered a hysterical curse on Enkidu, predicting fatefully that he would die young. Caught up short by this curse Gilgamesh wavered, but for the last time the enraged Enkidu drove him on. Gilgamesh thus finally killed Humbaba, slicing off his head with a single stroke.

After the battle Gilgamesh and Enkidu felt exhausted but heroic. As a symbol of their triumph they selected the tallest cedar tree in the forest and Gilgamesh cut it down. They planned to take this wood to the city of Nippur, and use it to produce a splendid new door for the temple. Other lesser trees were pressed into service as a raft, and with Enkidu steering their makeshift craft they started the long journey homeward, Gilgamesh holding in his lap the horrible head of Humbaba.

GILGAMESH SPURNS ISHTAR, AND THEY KILL THE BULL OF HEAVEN

The first task that met Gilgamesh on his return to Uruk was to try and clean himself up after the battle and the journeys. His hair was matted and his clothes filthy, so he washed at leisure and dressed again in regal garments, tying his sash and replacing the crown upon his head.

His very appearance, however, soon led him into difficulties, although this time it was not really Gilgamesh's fault. What happened was that Ishtar, the goddess of love, fell in love with him. It occurred the minute she set eyes on him, and in a long poetic speech she tried to woo the king, proposing that they should marry forthwith. His good fortune and his riches, she urged, would be beyond calculation.

Gilgamesh, however, was unmoved. Perhaps he didn't think her beautiful, or perhaps he was not in a marrying sort of mood, but he turned her down flat. He started off by insulting her outright, calling her names such as "pitch that blackens the hands of its bearer," or "a shoe that bites its owner's feet." Worse than that, Gilgamesh unwisely decided to bring up some of the things he knew about her past. In a long biting speech he spelled out the fate of her lover and husband, Tammuz, not to mention a certain shepherd, and even one of her father's gardeners, a man called Ishullanu. Each of these had once been loved by Ishtar, and each came to grief at her hands. Tammuz, for example, was condemned to an exhausting cycle of dying and rising again every year. The chief shepherd, who could not do enough for her, she turned into a wolf, so that his own assistant shepherds and dogs did not recognize

A goddess carved on a cylinder seal. The horned headdress shows that she is a goddess, not an ordinary woman. Ishtar often wore a headdress like this, with a long flounced dress and bracelets.

This image is another photomicrograph. The goddess figure on the seal itself is only 1 inch tall.

him, and chased him off. Ishullanu had resisted the goddess, and in a fit of anger she turned him into a frog, and made him live out his days in his own garden, with no one to turn him back into a man again. With such a record, Gilgamesh said, how could any woman expect to be seen as a suitable wife?

Ishtar was absolutely furious. She went straight up to heaven and rushed in to see her father Anu. Weeping and storming, she accused Gilgamesh of insulting her and slandering her. Anu was unimpressed. "What is all the fuss about? It was you who provoked King Gilgamesh in the first place, so that he talked about your despicable deeds and curses."

Ishtar took no notice of that. She demanded the Bull of Heaven from her father.

This Bull of Heaven was a magical and dangerous weapon. It was something that Anu would not give up lightly, especially into the hands of the hysterical Ishtar, who was bent on revenge. Once the Bull was set loose, it would inevitably mean death and destruction and seven years of hardship for all of Uruk. Had Ishtar reckoned with this, he asked, and laid in provisions for the innocent people in the city?

Ishtar brushed this aside, saying she had thought of all that, and that if Anu did not hand over the Bull right now, she would knock down the Underworld Gates. This was no idle threat, because it meant that the dead could come up and eat living people, and cause all kinds of complications for everybody. Once he learned that provision really had been made for the people below, Anu placed the Bull's reins in Ishtar's hand. She marched it off down to earth, making haste for Uruk, to avenge herself on Gilgamesh.

Anu's hesitation in unleashing the Bull of Heaven had been quite justified. After Ishtar and the Bull arrived at the city the beast gave a single snort, and a pit yawned in the ground: in fell 100 young men from Uruk. It snorted again, and a second pit claimed 200 young men. An even bigger chasm resulted from the third snort, and this time Enkidu himself fell in. Bravely he jumped out, and seized the Bull of Heaven by its horns. Angrily the Bull spat and swung his great tail dangerously.

A bull's head of lapis lazuli and gold. The bull was always regarded as an image of power and strength in ancient Mesopotamia. Bulls are often shown with beards or even with human heads (you can see one in the picture on page 26).

This bull's head decorated the sound box of a popular musical instrument called a lyre. Archaeologists found it in a royal Sumerian grave.

Once again Gilgamesh and Enkidu found themselves side by side in battle with a monstrous enemy. Shouting instructions to one another they agreed on tactics. Enkidu grabbed the tail and hung on for dear life, slowing up the Bull, while Gilgamesh seized his moment and, like a veteran bullfighter, struck the death-blow with his trusty sword. As a gesture of piety, they ripped out the Bull's heart as it lay there, and offered it to the Sun God.

Ishtar could hardly believe what had happened. She climbed up on the city wall and pronounced an ominous curse: "Woe to Gilgamesh who slandered me and killed the Bull of Heaven!"

Stung into fury, Enkidu impulsively ripped off one of the Bull's hindquarters and hurled it in Ishtar's face. "If only I could get at you I would do the same to you. I would drape his guts over your arms!" he cried.

Ishtar made a great show of mourning over the dead Bull's body, bringing her priestesses and servants to weep with her.

Gilgamesh, on the other hand, fetched the best craftsmen to inspect the corpse, drawing their attention especially to the vast horns, which were made of lapis lazuli. He had these hung up as a trophy on the wall in the palace.

Gilgamesh and Enkidu washed their bloodied hands in the waters of the river Euphrates. After that they marched triumphantly about the streets of Uruk, demanding, "Who is the bravest of the men? Who is the boldest of the males?" As you will readily imagine, Gilgamesh answered this question himself, shouting out his own name. A party was held to celebrate their victory and triumph. All enjoyed the merrymaking far into the night, and finally dropped off to untroubled sleep on the palace couches.

Enkidu, however, had a terrifying dream.

Gilgamesh and Enkidu slaying the Bull of Heaven – a seal and its impression. Like many bulls in Mesopotamian pictures, this one has a beard. Because it is a creature who lives in heaven it is also shown with wings. Enkidu (on the right) grasps the Bull by its tail, while Gilgamesh plunges his sword into its head. To the side you can see Ishtar, wearing a tall hat.

ENKIDU PAYS THE PRICE

Enkidu's dream was very ominous indeed. In it he saw the most important gods, agitated by these recent events, holding a conference in heaven. They discussed the rights and wrongs of what had happened. Anu declared that either Gilgamesh or Enkidu must die for killing Humbaba and the Bull of Heaven and cutting down the tallest cedar in the forest. Enlil spoke up for Gilgamesh, saying that Enkidu must be the one to pay. Then Shamash declared that Gilgamesh had been responsible for suggesting the whole thing in the first place, so how could they let innocent Enkidu take the blame in such a dreadful way?

Enkidu awoke to tell Gilgamesh about this dream, and now he lay sick.

Gilgamesh, in tears, protested aloud against the idea that Enkidu should be punished on his behalf, and Enkidu, reflecting bitterly that he was soon to become a ghost, moaned that he had not actually cut the fatal cedar for the temple door that had got them into such trouble.

Suddenly the ailing Enkidu caught sight of the door in question. He cursed it and lamented that he had ever selected the wood, or that he had helped to carry it back, or lavished attention on the sacred construction. It would have been better, he said, if he had seized an axe, and reduced it to planks for a raft.

Such talk distressed Gilgamesh even further. Trying to put things in perspective, he suggested that the mind of a strong hero should not be so readily disturbed by a mere dream, and that anyway he would himself beseech the gods for mercy. He would offer, too, a golden statue of Enkidu to the gods to try to soften Enlil's judgement, and overturn his grim sentence. Temporarily pacified, Enkidu fell into an uneasy sleep.

With the approach of dawn, however, Enkidu was once more overwhelmed with grief and depression. Lying weakly in the early light he began to think over his own story, and in a second burst of resentment he called upon Shamash to bring misfortune upon the wretched trapper who had first been responsible for involving him in his present circumstances. Then it occurred to Enkidu that his undoing was all Shamhat's fault, and he cursed her too. Enkidu wished all manner of unhappiness on poor Shamhat, until Shamash, who was listening sympathetically from heaven to all his outpourings, was moved to defend her. "But for her," said Shamash, "you would never have formed your friendship with Gilgamesh and enjoyed all those adventures at his side. And now at least Gilgamesh is preparing to do you great honor after your death, making a wonderful statue of you. Gilgamesh himself will certainly mourn you inconsolably, wandering the wilderness with matted hair, dressed in a lion's skin."

Enkidu was deeply affected by Shamash's words. He mused over them, and felt his anger drain away. Before long he heard himself speaking in a quite opposite way, invoking a blessed future for Shamhat, predicting that her beauty would be famed far and wide, and that men of all walks of life would fall in love with her.

Later, however, the troubled Enkidu lay with his insides in turmoil. Waking again, he told Gilgamesh of yet another dream, a dream even more full of foreboding. This time Enkidu found himself at the mercy of a fearsome creature, a mixture of eagle and lion, who evaded all Enkidu's attempts at attack, but pinioned him helplessly. Enkidu cried out to his friend to rescue him as usual, but Gilgamesh, he said, was afraid himself, and did not come forward.

Enkidu was then turned into a dove, and marched down to the underworld, where a very gloomy scene presented itself. The underworld, according to Enkidu's vision, was quite dark. Its inhabitants were dressed in dusty feathers, like birds, while all they had to eat and drink was clay and dirt; in fact there was dust everywhere. No one who had ended up in that place could get out again, and it was altogether far from cheerful.

When Enkidu arrived, the first thing he saw was a very sobering pile of old crowns from dead kings and rulers who no longer had any need for them. These former potentates were now employed serving the important gods with meals. (These, by the way, were real meals, involving meat, cakes, and lots of cool water from waterskins.) Many former priests were sitting about with no useful occupation. He even saw Ereshkigal, Queen of the Underworld, sitting on her throne in subterranean splendor, while in front of her another goddess called Belet-tseri was kneeling, holding a grim book called the "Tablet of Destinies."

The implications of this dream were unmistakable to Enkidu, even in his fevered condition, and Gilgamesh in his heart of hearts had to agree with him.

That was the last ominous dream that Enkidu had. He stayed in his bed, and day by day for twelve days he weakened and grew worse. Once he cried out in sudden anguish to his friend, the warrior king who had encouraged him so magnificently when he was afraid of Humbaba, and who, at the very moment when he was needed so desperately, was abandoning him.

Gilgamesh had little chance to soothe his beloved companion, or tell Enkidu that he would never abandon him. There was a dreadful noise in Enkidu's throat, and he fell silent forever.

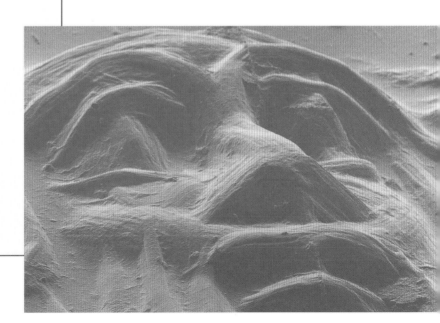

The suffering face of a hero from a cylinder seal, caught from an unusual angle.

TABLET THE EIGHTH

GILGAMESH LAMENTS OVER ENKIDU

Crouched at Enkidu's deathbed, watching as the sun rose, Gilgamesh was filled with melancholy. He spoke softly to Enkidu, talking about his early days in the countryside among the gazelles and donkeys, when he was fed on donkey's milk. The king summoned the world at large to mourn Enkidu's passing. Running over their adventures in his mind, he called upon friends and foes alike to mourn great Enkidu, calling upon the variety of fierce animals they knew, the countryside through which they passed, even the very roads that they had travelled, to join him in lamenting for Enkidu. His voice rose in a crescendo as he appealed to the Elders of Uruk to pay him heed in his grief.

> "Enkidu, my friend, the swiftest mule, fleetest wild donkey
>   of the mountain panther of the steppe-land,
> After we united our forces and went up into the mountain,
> Fought the Bull of Heaven, and killed him;
> Overwhelmed Humbaba, who lived in the Cedar Forest,
> What is this sleep that has now overtaken you?
> You have turned dark, and hear me not!"

Enkidu's eyes did not flicker, and when the speaker finally felt for a heartbeat, all was still. Tall Gilgamesh stooped over his immobile friend, and gently covered Enkidu's face with his cloak. Gilgamesh strode about the room like a lioness deprived of her cubs. Seizing his sword he hacked off his curls, and cast off his fine clothes. He had no need of such trappings, but was in deepest and most respectful mourning.

It was still early, but in a booming voice that echoed through the palace Gilgamesh summoned his craftsmen to start work on a statue of Enkidu. Skilled workers in metal and stone all came running to receive their instructions, and Gilgamesh described from head to foot his vision of the great memorial likeness, which was to be called "My Friend." The figure's chest was of lapis lazuli, and the skin was of beaten gold.

As Shamash had foretold, Gilgamesh put on the garments of a stricken mourner, roaming around the countryside dressed in a lion-skin. Often he addressed the spirit of Enkidu, calling out to remind his friend how Gilgamesh had done him honor as he had promised. Regularly he made offerings and gifts in memory of his companion.

One day in particular the grieving king made a decision. He rose early, and fetched out of the palace a special wooden table of which he was very proud. On it he placed a stone bowl of rich carnelian, which he filled with honey. Next to that he placed a lapis lazuli bowl, which he filled with butter. Raising his arms and his eyes to heaven he offered these symbolic riches to Shamash, the Sun God. Once again he would need divine protection, for Gilgamesh planned an even more desperate and unpredictable journey this time, inevitably, all alone in the face of unknown dangers.

GILGAMESH SETS OUT TO FIND THE SECRET OF ETERNAL LIFE

Something had changed inside Gilgamesh. While still weeping for his friend, going over and over Enkidu's death in his mind, he had begun to reflect bitterly on his own mortality. The realization that he, too, was doomed to die filled him with a powerful sense of resistance and rebellion. For Gilgamesh, you will recall, was not just a normal man. He was partly divine, and when he felt strongly about something, there was nothing that could deflect him from his purpose. Thus it came about that, after all his tribulations, Gilgamesh, King of Uruk, set out to find the secret of eternal life.

As Gilgamesh well knew, tradition recorded only one man had ever actually found eternal life, and that was Utnapishtim. Utnapishtim had been a king long long before Gilgamesh was born, ruling in another Sumerian city called Shuruppak. Utnapishtim alone had survived the Great Flood, the overwhelming waters that brought destruction upon the whole world, and he had been granted eternal life by the gods. Utnapishtim now lived with his wife in a very out-of-the-way place, right at the end of the world, called Mouth of the Rivers.

It seemed to Gilgamesh that he simply had to go and find Utnapishtim, and get the secret of eternal life directly from him. While thinking over this plan he had a dramatic and worrying dream, in which he arrived at a mountain pass at night only to meet a pair of lions, which he had to kill to save his own life. His journey was too important to put off, however, so despite some misgivings, Gilgamesh set off.

The journey turned out to be more trying than any of his previous expeditions, and when you consider that Enkidu was not by his side, his remarkable courage and perseverance seem all the greater.

After a long time Gilgamesh came to a vast mountain called Mashu. This was no ordinary mountain. It was located far beyond the horizon, and it guarded the place where the Sun rose and set. Here was a great gate, through which the fiery disc of the Sun would pass, and the gate itself was supervised by two very strange creatures called the Scorpion Beings. Theirs was a very responsible task, and they themselves were rather terrible to look at. In fact the poets say that the very sight of them meant death. This was because they could not permit any interference in their important daily work, and it suited them well to keep off possible troublemakers. Gilgamesh was not immune from fear, and their horrible appearance affected him as it would anyone else, so he started to tremble. However, being the hero he was, he overcame his fears, and marched boldly up to them.

Instantly the male Scorpion Being called to his mate, "The one who approaches, his body is of divine flesh!"

Just as promptly the female Scorpion Being replied, "Two-thirds of him may be divine, but one third is human."

Then the male Scorpion Being, speaking for both of them, called out to Gilgamesh to explain why he had come, and where exactly he thought he was going.

Gilgamesh retorted that he was seeking his ancestor Utnapishtim at Mouth of the Rivers, since he needed to talk over with him big questions about life and death.

This declaration came as a shock to the Scorpion Beings. No one had made that journey before as far as they knew, and no mortal would be able to do it. Why, there were twelve leagues of darkness across the mountain to deal with, and countless frightening challenges after that.

Gilgamesh listened to them politely, as he always did in such circumstances. When they had finished, he stated his case with such authority and determination that he convinced the Scorpion Beings to let him pass, and they opened their gate to him, even wishing him success on his venture.

Gilgamesh soon found himself thinking hard about what they had said to him. Following the road taken by the sun god he pressed on. Once he had traveled some distance he suddenly encountered a wall of impenetrable darkness. He could see neither ahead nor behind. Stepping delicately, closing his mind to fear, he walked steadily on. The first league fell behind him, then the second, then the third. He pressed on for twelve leagues in this nightmare blackness, entirely untouched by Shamash's rays, but unswerving and undaunted.

After twelve leagues' distance he stepped suddenly into brilliant light. Stumbling and blinking, he found himself outside a wonderful garden. As his eyes grew accustomed to the glare he made out that the trees were formed of precious stones. Carnelian grew as fruit – the branches were laden with dazzling clusters of it – and the leaves were of lapis lazuli. The spectacle was hard to take in, but delightful after the solitary darkness, and Gilgamesh felt his heart lift. Somewhat lightened, he walked on, to face whatever fate would bring him next.

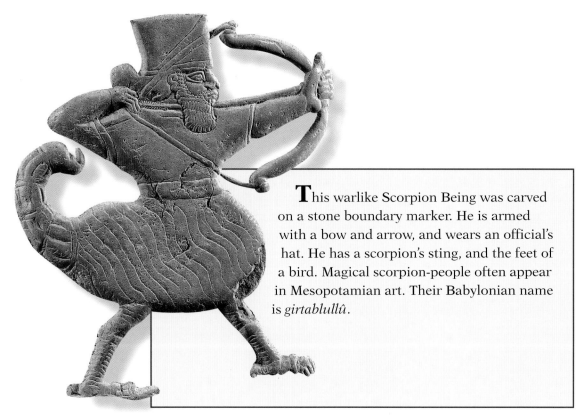

This warlike Scorpion Being was carved on a stone boundary marker. He is armed with a bow and arrow, and wears an official's hat. He has a scorpion's sting, and the feet of a bird. Magical scorpion-people often appear in Mesopotamian art. Their Babylonian name is *girtablullû*.

TABLET THE TENTH

GILGAMESH CROSSES THE WATERS OF DEATH

It was Siduri, who lived by the seashore, whom Gilgamesh encountered next. Siduri was a barmaid, and she had with her a special pot-stand and a fermenting vat to make beer, although no one really knows what she was doing there. When she saw Gilgamesh approaching she was alarmed by his haggard, mournful appearance, and thought he was likely to be dangerous. Acting swiftly she went into her house by the sea and slammed and locked her gate and door.

The loud noise startled Gilgamesh out of a reverie, and he looked up, realising what she had done. It annoyed him considerably. You can hardly blame him for this reaction, under the circumstances. He had just been through a particularly trying time, preoccupied with a serious and weighty project involving life and death, and was meaning no harm to anybody. It must be recorded that he stormed over to Siduri and asked just what she meant by her behavior. If she didn't open the door (and fast), he threatened, he would break down the door and smash the lock to bits as well.

He certainly caught Siduri's attention by this tactic. Gingerly she opened the door to him, and listened to what he had to say for himself. He revealed that he was Gilgamesh, that same well-known Gilgamesh who had killed Humbaba, Guardian of the Cedar Forest, and slain lions in the mountains, not to mention also the Bull of Heaven, who had come down from heaven specially to get him. Siduri looked at him steadily. She was skeptical and asked him why, if he really was Gilgamesh, he looked so sad and exhausted.

Gilgamesh answered her questions at length. His voice was no longer strident and angry, but hushed and reflective. He explained to Siduri why it was that he looked the way he did, mourning for his beloved Enkidu, and smitten with the knowledge of his own mortality.

Saddened herself, Siduri thought over his words, imagining what lay ahead in the comfortless life Gilgamesh had chosen. Moved to pity she replied to him:

"Gilgamesh, where are you wandering?
The life that you are seeking all around you will not find.
When the gods created mankind they fixed death for
mankind but life they held back in their own hands.
Now you, Gilgamesh, let your belly be full!
Be happy day and night, make each day into a party!
Dance in circles day and night!
Let your clothes be spotless, let your head be clean; wash
yourself with water!
Look after the little one who holds you by the hand,
Let a wife delight in your embrace!
This is what human beings are supposed to do."

Gilgamesh heard the words of the barmaid, but they had no power to move him. On the contrary, when she had finished speaking he asked her doggedly about the route to find Utnapishtim, and what markers he might use to recognize whether he were on the right path. Be it across the sea, or through the wilderness, he was determined to go on.

Siduri responded sadly. "O Gilgamesh, there has never been any way across the sea, not since the remotest times. No one but the Sun God, Shamash, can cross the Waters of Death."

Gilgamesh felt a tremor when he heard of the Waters of Death, but then Siduri told him that there was a special ferryman. This ferryman was called Urshanabi, and he acted as a servant to Shamash the Sun God. According to Siduri, however, to cross the Waters of Death in safety it was necessary to have possession of the Things-of-Stone. She couldn't explain what they were exactly (no more can I, as a matter of fact), but she did know that they were essential for safe navigation across those deadly waters.

The obvious solution was to find Urshanabi and discuss it with him. Siduri pointed out that he was picking some edible plant in the woods, the Things-of-Stone by his side.

"Go on, let him see your face," she urged Gilgamesh. "If possible, you should cross over with him. If not, you should turn back now."

By this stage Gilgamesh, however, had become something close to hysterical. Rather than approaching Urshanabi with a reasonable request for help, he took axe and dagger in hand, stealthily crept by him in the forest, and attacked the "Things-of-Stone" where they lay. Urshanabi came running, but he was too late to save them from destruction. Urshanabi, appalled, demanded to know who the attacker was. Again Gilgamesh's anger abated, and he answered at length, explaining in the same words he had used to Siduri who he was, why his appearance was so strained and drawn, and what he was desperately hunting for.

Gilgamesh asked Urshanabi the way to find Utnapishtim, and requested a description of the markers that would show him his route.

Urshanabi did not mince his words, but blamed Gilgamesh to his face for destroying the very items that would be needed. The Things-of-Stone were the markers, and now they were hopelessly smashed. Even the ropes that held them were cut to ribbons. The only way left now, he said, was to go into the forest and cut wood. He would need three hundred punting poles each 60 cubits in length. The poles would have to be stripped of their bark, and smoothed all over, and provided with caps at the end. The moment Gilgamesh heard this he went straight into the forest and started work, this time putting his axe and dagger to constructive use. Soon he was back with the three hundred poles, prepared exactly according to Urshanabi's instructions.

The two climbed into Urshanabi's boat, and put to sea. After three days they had sailed the distance that would have taken a normal man a month and a half, and this brought them to the Waters of Death. Urshanabi explained the necessary procedure. It would be fatal, he explained, if Gilgamesh's hands were to touch the water at any time. The technique was to employ the poles one by one as punts, and as one slipped from his grasp he was to use the next, and so on, remembering at all times to avoid the splash and the spray.

UTNAPISHTIM

This clay tablet shows a map of the mythological world drawn by a scribe in about 600 BC.
In the middle is the city of Babylon. The known world is surrounded by a ring of water. Beyond that are the regions where figures from mythology were thought to live – they are represented by triangles rising from the sea. The cuneiform text at the top says that Utnapishtim the Faraway lived in one of these regions. The text also mentions the Scorpion Beings.

Before long all the poles had been used up. Undaunted Gilgamesh stripped off his shirt and held it between outstretched hands as a makeshift sail.

Utnapishtim, on the other side, was standing on the shore, gazing out across the waters and daydreaming. Suddenly he made out a gaunt silhouette against the sky, and noticed at once that the Things-of-Stone that belonged to the boat were in fragments. He knew too that the figure he saw holding the sail was no one he recognized, and certainly not someone who should properly be arriving with Urshanabi.

As they came close Gilgamesh answered Utnapishtim's unspoken enquiry and revealed his identity. He did not realize who Utnapishtim was. Again Gilgamesh explained as he had before why his appearance was so strained and drawn, and what he was desperately hunting for. "That is why," said Gilgamesh, "I must proceed to see Utnapishtim, whom they call Faraway."

Utnapishtim listened gravely to Gilgamesh's speech, considering carefully what his unexpected visitor had told him. Then he too began to speak, a profound speech, full of wisdom, of unanswerable logic, and based on infinite knowledge of man and his destiny. He agreed that a certain period of grief for another was wholesome, but he argued that it was always man's responsibility to make the most of his life. The span of human life itself was all too short, and human accomplishments that might seem significant or far-reaching were themselves fleeting:

"For how long can we build a household?
For how long can we seal a document?
For how long can brothers share an inheritance?"

Mundane preoccupations are only mundane, came the steady, ageless voice, and there was no escape from man's inevitable destiny:

"Suddenly there is nothing!
How similar are a prisoner and a dead man!
Death itself cannot be depicted
But mankind is indeed imprisoned."

Human beings, said Utnapishtim, could never gain mastery over Death. After the Flood, the gods laid down the rules concerning Death and Life. One thing they did not do, was to divulge the secret of man's allotted days.

As his voice sank to a whisper it came to Gilgamesh for the first time that the speaker before him was none other than Utnapishtim the Faraway himself.

THE STORY
OF THE FLOOD, AND THE
END OF THE QUEST

What had confused Gilgamesh at first was the fact that Utnapishtim the Faraway looked like any other man, even a bit like Gilgamesh himself. His appearance had rather disarmed the warrior king, whose original plan had been to fight Utnapishtim in order to wrest his secret from him. If then, asked the wearied Gilgamesh, the gods had resolved to keep the secret of immortality for themselves, how was it that Utnapishtim, a man like himself, had been granted eternal life?

Utnapishtim the Faraway braced himself for a lengthy narrative. It had been a long time since anyone had come to ask him his story, and probably he was quite glad to have Gilgamesh as an audience. Also, technically, the matter was a secret of the gods, but it was clear to Utnapishtim that these were special circumstances.

The story began long ago, in the ancient city of Shuruppak on the bank of the River Euphrates. For some reason (perhaps because of all the noise they had to endure) the Great Gods decided to send a flood to wipe out mankind. It was a closely-guarded secret, and only such gods as counselor Enlil, chamberlain Ninurta, or canal specialist Ennugi, knew what was afoot.

Another god in the know was Ea, but either he disagreed with the plan or was simply highly indiscreet, because he passed a message on by whispering to the reeds that made up the walls of Utnapishtim's house:

A reed house like those of ancient Sumer. People living in the marshes of southern Iraq were still building houses like this from bundles of reeds up till modern times.

The houses are called *mudhif* in Arabic.

"Reed hut! Reed hut! Wall! Wall!
Reed hut, listen! Reed hut, reflect!
O man of Shuruppak, son of Ubartutu
Tear down the house and build a boat!
Abandon wealth and seek living beings!
Spurn possessions and keep living beings alive!
Make all living beings go up into the boat!"

Ea confided to Utnapishtim the necessary dimensions and proportions for the extraordinary boat which he was to build. Since this was clearly a matter of divine instruction Utnapishtim naturally agreed to do as he was bid, but it occurred to him that his subjects would wonder what on Earth he was up to. How should he answer their quizzing, he asked? Ea's answer was for him to say that Enlil had rejected him, so that he could neither live happily in Shuruppak, nor indeed anywhere else on the Earth supervised by Enlil, so he was planning on descending to live in a boat on the Apsu. (These were the great subterranean waters that all ancient Mesopotamians knew were gathered beneath the Earth itself.) This answer satisfied Utnapishtim, so early the following morning work on the boat began. Specialist craftsmen such as carpenters and reed-workers were recruited, and even children in the family were set to carrying pitch to seal the timbers and make the boat watertight.

The boat itself was as large as a field, and, most remarkably, square in shape. Utnapishtim planned out the work carefully, and prepared a drawing to use as a guide if they got confused. The boat needed six decks and seven levels, subdivided into nine compartments. The quantities of pitch required were enormous, and there were other lavish demands, since Utnapishtim was determined to keep his workmen happy, and gave them excellent food and lots of drink. Given this, you will not be surprised to hear that the great construction was completed by sunset that very day.

Launching the craft was very tricky. They built a slipway of poles, and it was a difficult job collecting the used poles from the back and dashing to lay them down in front in time. Once the front section had run into the water, Utnapishtim began the second part of his great task, which was loading it with its unusual cargo. First he took on board all the wordly riches he could gather.

There are at least 120,000 clay tablets from ancient Mesopotamia in the British Museum, but this one is probably the most famous of them all. Although it is broken, it gives a large portion of Tablet the Eleventh of our story, telling the story of the Flood. This tablet was deciphered over 120 years ago by an Assyriologist called George Smith. Smith was thrilled when he realized that what he had read was related to the story of Noah in the Bible. Another scholar in the Museum described how Smith "jumped up and rushed around the room in a great state of excitement, and to the astonishment of those present, began to undress himself."

Then, much more importantly, he turned to the question of living beings. He loaded all the living beings into the boat, his family, the craftsmen, and all the beasts and animals of the field.

Shamash had promised to give him a signal to indicate that everybody had to be aboard, and the entrance sealed from within. Once that sign had been given the weather turned, just before Utnapishtim sealed the door.

A great black cloud rose from the horizon, thunder rumbled, and the earth was overwhelmed with floodwater and fire. Gods and men alike were stunned, and the human beings left behind had no chance of survival and were submerged in the water. The gods who lived in shrines on earth were terrified, and departed, retreating to the safety of heaven. Many were to be seen there cowering like dogs against the wall, while above the roar the goddess Ishtar could be heard wailing for the people, in anguished regret that her vote in the assembly had contributed to so disastrous a decision.

Flood and tempest raged for six days and seven nights. On the seventh day everything grew calm. Utnapishtim looked around. Everything was covered in water and totally silent; all the people had turned to clay. Utnapishtim wept. He gazed round the horizon, and could only distinguish one remote point sticking out of the sea.

The heavily laden vessel itself had come to rest on top of a mountain. This mountain was called Mount Nimush, and it gripped the boat in such a way that there was no movement. Utnapishtim kept close watch, but for six successive days there was no change. When the seventh day arrived Utnapishtim took one of his doves and released it out over the water, but it could find no perch, and flew back to him. He tried the same with a swallow, but back it came. Then he dispatched one of the ravens, and the raven saw the waters retreating, and found food, and a place to perch, so it did not return. Thereupon Utnapishtim released all the animals to find themselves new homes, and start their lives again. In gratitude he made offerings to the gods, who all flocked around eagerly since they had received no sacrifices for days. An important goddess was just making a speech to the effect that such a terrible day should never be forgotten, and declaring that Enlil should not partake of the offerings since the annihilation of the people was all his fault, when Enlil himself turned up, likewise attracted by the delicious smells of the offerings. When he saw the boat, and realized its implications, he was livid. No living being at all had been supposed to escape. Learning that Ea was responsible for interfering he was about to turn on him when Ea spoke up, forestalling him.

Ea asked quietly how someone described as the Sage of the Gods could have possibly behaved in such a way. Better, he said, that lions, or wolves, or famine, or even plague had come on the population rather than such a flood that would kill everybody indiscriminately.

Finally, Ea claimed that he had not given out secret information as such, but that he had merely been responsible for sending a dream.

Ea's clever words calmed Enlil, who deftly thought of a way to save face. Marching up the gangplank into the boat, he seized Utnapishtim's hand, brought his wife close, and blessing them both, made them immortal:

"Previously Utnapishtim was a human being,
But now let Utnapishtim and his wife become like us, the gods!
Let Utnapishtim dwell far distant, at Mouth of the Rivers."

"So that is what happened," said Utnapishtim to Gilgamesh, winding up the story, "and here we have been ever since."

If Gilgamesh wanted immortality, he continued, there was a difficulty. Who would call the gods together and propose such an idea? Meanwhile, he suggested a test, to see if Gilgamesh were really of the right stuff to be regarded as a serious candidate. The test was that Gilgamesh was not to lie down and sleep for six days and seven nights. (This, you will remember, was the period that Utnapshtim had to stay awake during the Flood, so he knew what was involved.)

Poor exhausted Gilgamesh. The minute he sat down, he fell into a fog-like sleep. Utnapishtim's wife looked at him with compassion. She wanted her husband to wake him gently and send him home, but Utnapishtim was not so soft, and ridiculed the idea that such a sleeper would consider himself a potential immortal. He told his wife to bake some loaves, and set one by his head for each day he slept, so they could prove the length of his sleep when he finally awoke. Gilgamesh slept for seven days, whereupon Utnapishtim touched him. Gilgamesh awoke, and said immediately, "I was not asleep! You woke me just as I was dropping off!"

Utnapishtim was having none of that, but showed him the seven loaves, and how they varied between being dry, stale, moist, white or moldy, depending on their age. Gilgamesh was utterly crestfallen:

"O Woe! What shall I do, Utnapishtim, where shall I go?
The Snatcher Demon has grabbed my flesh,
in my very bedroom dwells Death.
and wherever I set foot there too is Death!"

Utnapishtim had suddenly had his fill of Gilgamesh's company. He cursed the ferryman Urshanabi, and told him to take Gilgamesh away, clean him up, dress him properly, set him on the homeward path, and make sure that he did, indeed, go home. Urshanabi, of course, did as he was bid. He helped Gilgamesh to freshen himself up and the two of them boarded his boat and sailed away.

Just after they had gone Utnapishtim's wife felt very guilty. She told her husband that they really ought have given Gilgamesh something to enable him to return home honorably from his quest for immortality, in view of his state of mind. Gilgamesh heard this, and swiftly brought the boat back to the shore. Utnapishtim then told him of a certain hidden plant, rather like a boxthorn, that would prick him like a rose. "Touch that plant with your own hands," he said, "and you will be as a young man again."

The magic plant lay far below, deep in the underground waters of the Apsu. To get to it Gilgamesh had to weight his feet with sharp and painful stones. The plant did indeed prick his hands, but he grasped it, regaining the surface in triumph in a stream of bubbles. He did not use it at once on himself, but showed the plant to Urshanabi. Since the plant's name was An-Old-Man-Becomes-A-Young-Man, he proposed trying it out on the oldest man in Uruk as soon as they got back to the city.

They made their customary speed through the day, but when they eventually stopped for the night Gilgamesh yielded to a whim and bathed in the waters of a cool spring. While he was engaged in doing this, a snake smelled the delicious aroma of the magic plant, and stealthily approached, carrying it off and eating it. Gilgamesh returned just in time to see it sloughing its old skin, already rejuvenated by the plant's power.

Gilgamesh could only weep in frustration. He appealed to Urshanabi for counsel, desperate for some words of comfort, but none was forthcoming. All his efforts and sufferings had been in vain!

Losing no further time after this disaster, Gilgamesh and Urshanabi sped back to Uruk.

When they arrived, Gilgamesh felt an unexpected sense of peace sweep over him, and even a sense of pride in the noble city of which he was king. He sent Urshanabi up on the famous walls to walk around, and get an idea of the city, its spaciousness, its beauty, and its great age.

"Those walls," he said, gesturing, "were built by the Seven Sages themselves." Urshanabi looked suitably impressed, and stole a glance at his troublesome but adventurous passenger. There was no doubt, he thought, that king Gilgamesh looked happier back here in Uruk than he had for ages.

This snake was carved on a Babylonian boundary-marker, to protect the marker and its message.

Important Names in the Story

ANU	chief god worshipped by the ancient Mesopotamians.
EA	third major god, kinder and less conventional than other gods, with a good sense of humor.
ENKIDU	the wild man who grew up among animals and became Gilgamesh's great friend and companion.
ENLIL	second major god, rather serious, and responsible for organizing much of the Mesopotamian universe.
GILGAMESH	the hero of the story, the brave king of Uruk who set out to achieve immortality.
ISHTAR	the goddess of love, daughter of Anu. An explosive and impulsive character of strong affections and emotions.
LUGALBANDA	according to some, Gilgamesh's father.
SHAMASH	the Sun God.
SHAMHAT	the beautiful young girl who taught Enkidu about love and humanity.
SIDURI	the barmaid who lived at the end of the world.
URSHANABI	the ferryman who daily navigated Shamash safely across the Waters of Death.
UTNAPISHTIM	an ancient king who, like Noah, built a great boat to rescue living creatures when the gods sent the Flood.

Further Reading

The world of Ancient Mesopotamia, for children:
L. Oakes, *The Assyrians Activity Book*, British Museum Press, 1995.
P. Harper, *Writing Activity Book*, British Museum Press, 1996.
(includes information on cuneiform writing)

Friendly translations of the whole story can be found in:
M. V. Kovacs, *The Epic of Gilgamesh*, Stamford University Press, 1989.
S. Dalley, *Myths from Mesopotamia*, Oxford University Press, 1989.
A. George, *The Epic of Gilgamesh*, Penguin, 1998.

Cuneiform writing, for adults:
C. B. F. Walker, *Cuneiform*, British Museum Press, 1987.

The Pictures

All the objects illustrated are from the collections of the British Museum.

page 1	Lion from cylinder seal, WAA 113871
page 5 *above*	Assyrian relief, WAA 124875
page 5 *below*	Cuneiform tablet, WAA K225+
page 6	Hero from cylinder seal, WAA 113871
page 13	Clay model: face of Humbaba, WAA 116624
page 16	Impression of cylinder seal, WAA 89115
page 20	Seal and impression, WAA 89763
page 23	Goddess from cylinder seal, WAA 89271
page 25	Head of bull from Sumerian lyre, WAA 121198A
page 26	Seal and impression, WAA 89435
page 29	Hero from cylinder seal, WAA 89111
page 34	Scorpion-Being from stone boundary-marker, WAA 90858
page 38	Cuneiform tablet, WAA 92687
page 41	Reed house in southern Iraq, Victoria Theakston/Robert Harding Picture Library
page 42	Cuneiform tablet, WAA K3375
page 46	Snake from stone boundary-marker, WAA 90841